Strawberry Shortcake Characters and Designs © 1983 American Greetings Corporation. TM* designates trademarks of American Greetings Corporation.

Library of Congress Cataloging in Publication Data: Rosenblatt, Arthur S. Strawberry Shortcake and the deep, dark woods.
SUMMARY: Strawberry Shortcake thinks that she has lost her way in the forest, but soon finds her way home with help from an unexpected source.
[1. Lost children—Fiction] I. Sustendal, Pat, ill.
II. Title. PZ7.R71916St 1983 [E] 83-8091 ISBN 0-910313-07-5
Manufactured in the United States of America   2 3 4 5 6 7 8 9 0

Strawberry Shortcake

and the Deep, Dark Woods

Story by Arthur S. Rosenblatt
Pictures by Pat Sustendal

Strawberry Shortcake sat down next to Custard and looked at her neat and tidy strawberry patch. She had just finished weeding and watering every single berry plant. They now stood clean and clear, nodding in the golden sunlight.

Strawberry was pleased that she had finished so quickly, and decided to do something special with the rest of her day.

"Custard," she said, "I have a wonderful idea. Let's fill a basket with some strawberries. Then we'll invite all our friends for a picnic lunch in the woods. While we're there, we can pick some pretty wildflowers for our supper table. Won't that be fun?"

While Strawberry filled the basket, Custard frolicked about. Her wavy tail sometimes twined about the picnic basket and once it almost spilled the berries!

"Now we're ready," said Strawberry, as she laid a clean white napkin on top of the berries. And off they went.

Their first stop was just across the valley at the big house with the flaky blue shutters. Strawberry marched up and tapped on the slightly topsy-turvy door. Her friend and closest neighbor, Huckleberry Pie, opened it. Strawberry saw that he had dripping wet hands. His dog, Pupcake, stood at his side, wagging his striped tail back and forth.

"Well, well, well," he said, "Hello, Strawberry. I was just splashing some water on my huckleberries to keep them fresh."

"And splashing yourself, too," thought Strawberry. But she didn't say so to him. Huckleberry really tried hard and meant well, even if he was a bit messy.

"I'm going off to the forest for a picnic lunch, Huckleberry. Would you like to come with me?" she asked.

"Aw, gee, Strawberry, I was just getting ready to go fishing with Pupcake down at the Strawberry Soda Stream. I hear the candy trout are jumping. Maybe next time."

It was the same story at every house. Everyone had something else to do.

Raspberry Tart had slept late and had too many chores left.

"So much to do," said Raspberry, "that I can't just go off whenever I want. Besides, Rhubarb is being naughty. Rhubarb!" she called, "You come right down off that roof."

Even Blueberry Muffin couldn't come.

"Today is my baking day," she explained. "Even when the sun shines, I have to get my blueberry goodies into the oven."

Her pet mouse, Cheesecake, licked the crumbs off her face and nodded her head.

"Well," said Strawberry Shortcake to Custard as they headed down the lane, "we'll just go by ourselves. But let's fill the basket so full of wildflowers that we can give some to everyone when we get back. That will be a nice surprise for them."

In no time at all, they arrived at a clearing deep in the woods. Strawberry nibbled on some of the sweet, juicy berries and gave Custard a little cup of milk which she had brought along.

Then she looked around.
There were starchy white
daisies swaying gently in
the breeze. Clusters of

lemon yellow buttercups opened
their petals in a cheerful
greeting. Tiny bluebells peeked
out from behind lacy ferns.

While Custard chased after a fluttering butterfly, Strawberry filled her basket to the top with the most beautiful flowers.

After so much work, both Strawberry and Custard were
quite tired.

"I'll just close my eyes for a short nap," said Strawberry,
"and then we'll go home."

They lay down at the edge of the clearing on a soft bed of
pine needles. Strawberry used a clump of velvet green moss as
a pillow and soon fell fast asleep.

A cool breeze tickling her chin told Strawberry it was time
to wake up. And, sure enough, the sun had disappeared
somewhere behind the trees. Right over there. Or was it there?
She just wasn't sure. From far off, Strawberry heard the
hoot-hoot of an owl. She knew it was time to be on their way.

Custard padded along the stony path as they set off in one direction. Before long they came to a great big hill. Strawberry knew they had never seen it before.

"Oh, dear, this must be the wrong way. We'd better turn around," she said.

They trudged on as it grew darker and darker.

Twisting vines seemed to reach out to trip them. Jagged rocks and fallen logs seemed to grow up right in the middle of their way. Suddenly, there was a gigantic lake in front of them. It was so big, they couldn't even see the other side.

Strawberry began to get a little scared, but she knew she had to be brave for Custard. "We can't cross here, Custard. We'll just have to keep trying until we find a path that leads us home. Here," she said, as she leaned down to pick him up. "You seem so tired, I'll carry you for a while."

Even though she was weary herself, Strawberry marched
forward through the deep, dark woods. As she walked, she
began to think that they were really lost.

Just then she heard a buzzing near her ear.
Through the dim light she could just make out
the tiny speckled body and wings of Lucky Bug,
hovering right in front of her.

"Lucky Bug, how glad I am to see you! Did you come out to join us? You know you're always welcome. But it's so dark now. Do you think you could show us the way home?" Strawberry asked.

Lucky Bug buzzed happily, circled round and then flew off. Suddenly, ahead on the path, there were hundreds of sparkling dots of light. And in the center was Lucky Bug! She had gathered her friends, the fireflies, to form a big ball of light.

Custard jumped down and gaily trotted after them, and Strawberry skipped merrily behind.

They followed the dancing light through the dark trees and bushes and soon came to the edge of the forest. There in the distance, with the moonlight now shining down, was Strawberry's own strawberry patch and cosy home.

"I can hardly wait to get there so that we can have our supper," said Strawberry Shortcake as she waved goodbye to the friendly fireflies.

And in a twinkling, she was home. She opened the door, and what a surprise! Seated at the table were Huckleberry Pie, Raspberry Tart and Blueberry Muffin, with plates of candy trout, crisp tarts and hot, crumbly muffins set out in front of them.

"We thought a supper all together would be fun," said Raspberry Tart.

Custard ran to join Pupcake, Rhubarb and Cheesecake
playing in front of the fireplace as Strawberry rushed forward
to greet her friends.

"Wherever have you been so long? We've been waiting for you. Has anything happened?" asked Blueberry Muffin.

"Oh, nothing much," laughed Strawberry Shortcake. "I went into the forest to pick some wildflowers and ended up finding some new friends. And," she added, "one special old friend as well."

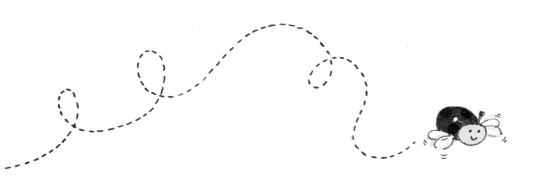

With a happy buzzing near her ear, Strawberry Shortcake then sat down to celebrate her return. She gave a flower to everyone, ate some of the good things on the table and then finished up with a glass of milk and a big bowl of her favorite fruit, bright red, delicious strawberries.

"This has been a 'berry' exciting day," said Strawberry. "But being with all my friends is the 'berry' best part of all."